Pants and More Pants

PANTS AND MORE PANTS
A DAVID FICKLING BOOK 978 1 849 92051 3

First published in Great Britain by David Fickling Books
an imprint of Random House Children's Books
A Random House Group Company

This edition published 2010

PANTS first published in Great Britain by David Fickling Books, 2002
MORE PANTS first published in Great Britain by David Fickling Books, 2007

1 3 5 7 9 10 8 6 4 2

DAVID FICKLING BOOKS
31 Beaumont Street, Oxford, OX1 2NP

www.rbooks.co.uk
www.kidsatrandomhouse.co.uk

Addresses for companies within The Random House Group Limited can be found
at: www.randomhouse.co.uk/offices.htm

THE RANDOM HOUSE GROUP Limited Reg. No. 954009

A CIP catalogue record for this book is available from the British Library
Printed in China

Pants and More Pants

Giles Andreae

Nick Sharratt

David Fickling Books

Pants

Small pants, big pants

Giant frilly pig pants

New pants, blue pants one, two, three

Pants you can wear if you're ten feet tall!

Loose pants, tight pants

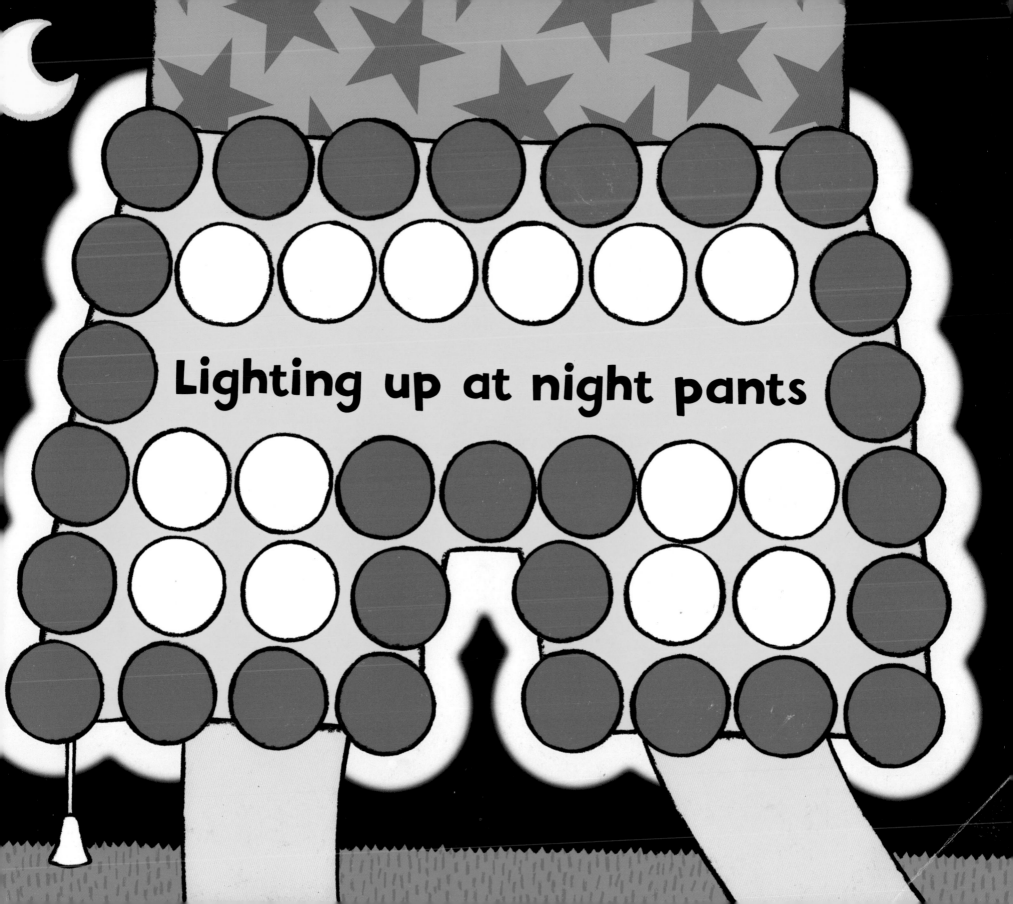

Lighting up at night pants

Black pants, white pants,

no pants at all!

Pants to pick a daisy, pants for being lazy

Pants on your head
when you've gone crazy!

Funny pants,
money pants

Wear them when it's sunny pants

Have you seen these bunny pants?

– yes I have!

Little baby nappy pants

Special pants for driving in the car!

Fairy pants, hairy pants

What a lot of lovely

pants there are!

More Pants

Red pants, green pants

Yellow submarine pants

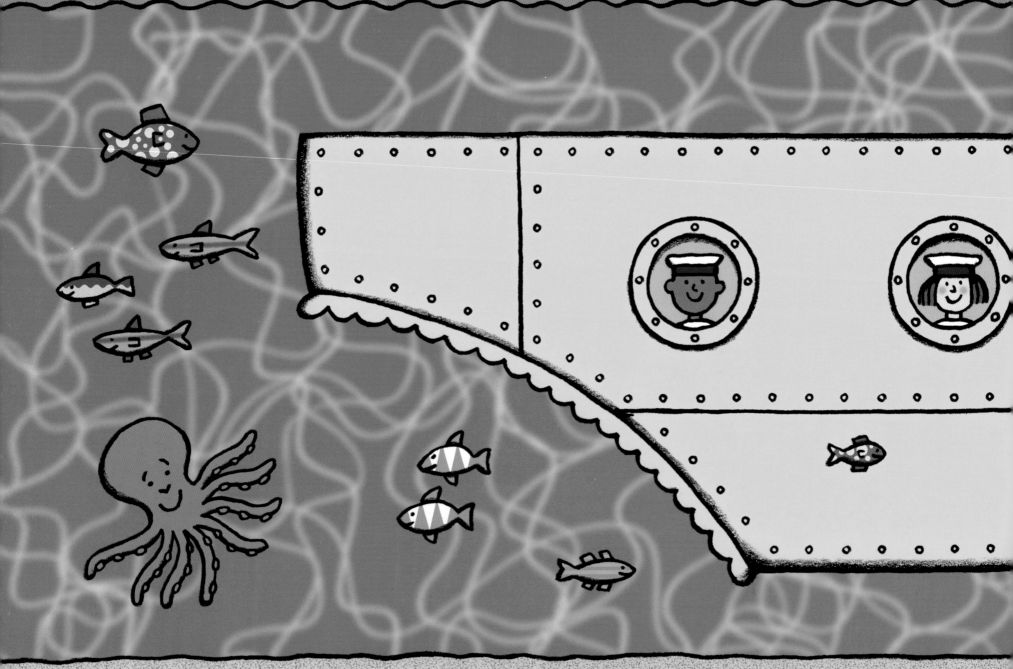

Tickling your tummy pants

And matching bra!

Arty pants,
party pants

Black belt in
karate pants

Have you done a farty pants?

Puffy pants,
fluffy pants

Pants
for a
scary
dinosaur

Colder pants,

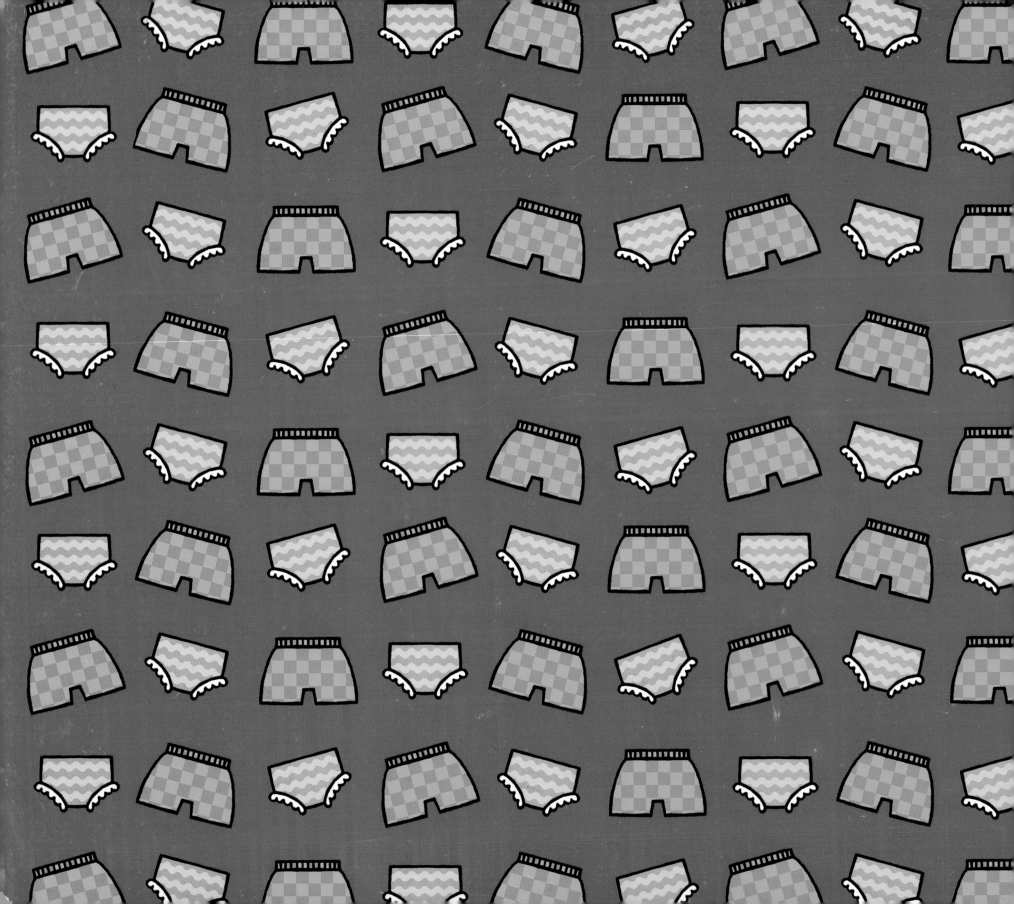

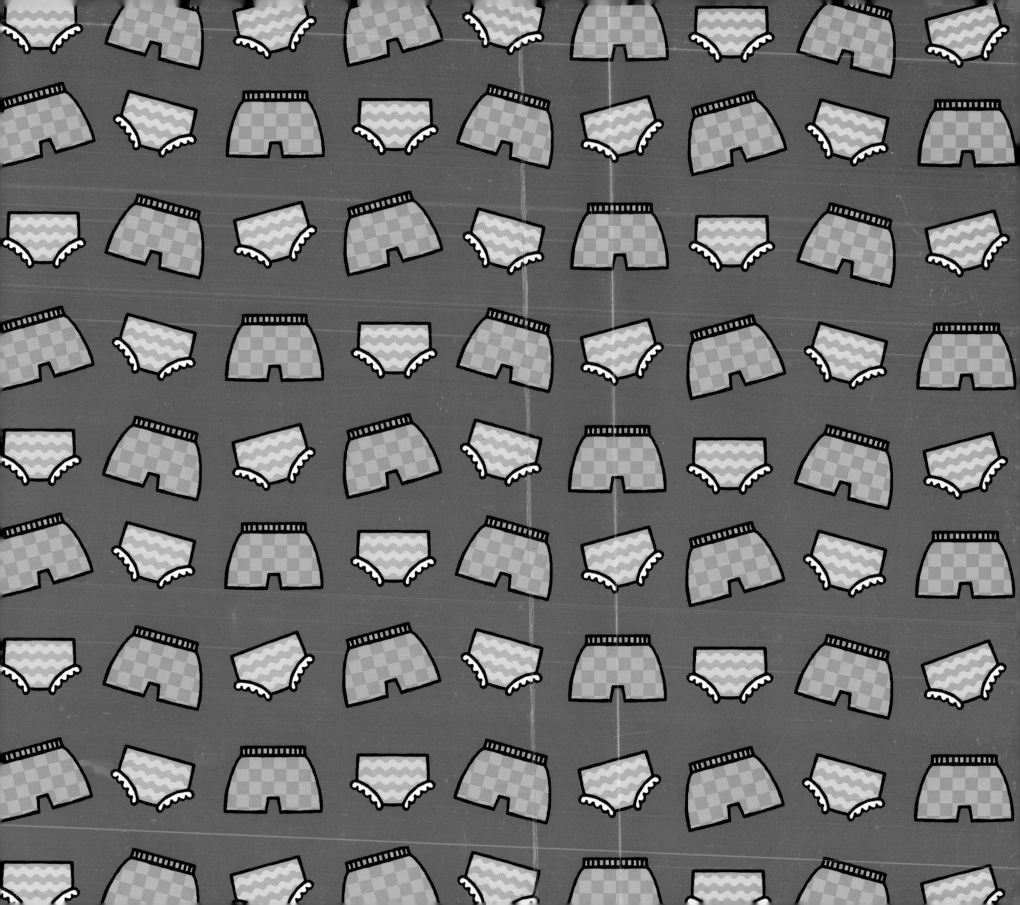